D0407308

Dora Helps Diego!

by Laura Driscoll
illustrated by Tom Mangano

Ready-to-Read

Simon Spotlight/Nick Jr.
New York   London   Toronto   Sydney

Hi! I am .

DORA

DIEGO, BOOTS, and I

need your help!

Oh, no! is missing!

BABY JAGUAR

 cannot find him!

DIEGO

 and I

BOOTS

are helping find him.

DIEGO

Will you help too?

Great!

Help us find  !

BABY JAGUAR

Look up in that .

TREE

I see a .

TAIL

 has a .

BABY JAGUAR   TAIL

Does it belong to ?

BABY JAGUAR

No.

It is a  SNAKE

getting out of the ☼. SUN

Where is **BABY JAGUAR**?

Look behind those .
FLOWERS

I see 🍼🍼.
FEET

has .

BABY JAGUAR FEET

Do they belong to  ?

BABY JAGUAR

No.

It is 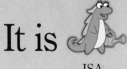 working in her .

ISA

GARDEN

Where is  ?
BABY JAGUAR

Look behind that trunk.

TREE

I see .

WHISKERS

 has ✱.

BABY JAGUAR   WHISKERS

Do those ✱ **belong**

WHISKERS

to **?**

BABY JAGUAR

No.

It is , that sneaky fox.
SWIPER

Where is  ?
BABY JAGUAR

Look behind the .
SLIDE

I see .
SPOTS

 has .

BABY JAGUAR   SPOTS

Do they belong to  ?

BABY JAGUAR

No.

It is the scarf that

belongs to .
BENNY

Will we **ever** find  ?
BABY JAGUAR

We need to go back to

the Animal Rescue Center.

We open the .

DOOR

We cannot believe it!

We see a  , ,
         TAIL   FEET

 , and .
WHISKERS   SPOTS

Here is !
         BABY JAGUAR

 is so happy!

DIEGO

We found !

BABY JAGUAR

Thanks for helping!

Diego Saves a Butterfly

adapted by Lara Bergen
based on the original teleplay by Madellaine Paxson
illustrated by Warner McGee

Ready-to-Read

SIMON SPOTLIGHT/NICK JR.
New York   London   Toronto   Sydney

Hi! I am  .
DIEGO

Look at this !
COCOON

Do you know what is inside?

It is a  !
BUTTERFLY

It is a Blue Morpho !
BUTTERFLY

"Let me see!" says .

BABY JAGUAR

Oh, no!

The  flew away.

BUTTERFLY

I think

BABY JAGUAR

scared the .

BUTTERFLY

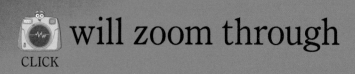 will zoom through

the rainforest to look for

the .

Is this the ?
BUTTERFLY

No, this is a .
LADYBUG

Is this the ?
BUTTERFLY

Yes!

BUTTERFLIES live
in the rainforest.
But this **BUTTERFLY**
is in a **CAVE**.
The **CAVE** is cold!

We have to bring the  BUTTERFLY

back to the warm rainforest.

Come on!

Now we are in the  .

But the 🕳 is so dark!

🎒 can help us see.

Here is !

Can help us see?

No.

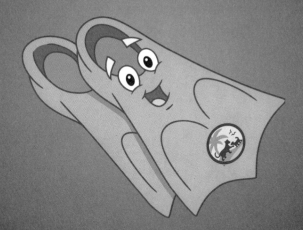

Can a help us see?

Yes!

There is the  !

BUTTERFLY

"I am too cold to fly,"
says the .
That is okay, .
You can ride with me.

 like to sip juice

BUTTERFLIES

from .

FRUIT

Do you see any  ?

FRUIT

"Yum!" says the .

BUTTERFLY

The 🥔 was good.

FRUIT

The 🦋 is warm

BUTTERFLY

again.

Now she can fly!

To the rainforest!

Come on!

Oh, no!

There is a big  !
BIRD

The is afraid of .
BUTTERFLY   BIRDS

When the  opens its
wings, the flies away.
The is brave!

We made it back
to the rainforest.
But where is  ?

BABY JAGUAR

"Here I am," says  .

BABY JAGUAR

"I do not want to

scare the .

BUTTERFLY

I want to be friends."

"Me too!" says the  .

BUTTERFLY

Thanks for helping us save the  !

BUTTERFLY

And thanks for helping

BABY JAGUAR

make a new friend too!

NICK JR.

DORA the EXPLORER®

Dora and the Baby Crab

by Kirsten Larsen   illustrated by Robert Roper

Ready-to-Read

Simon Spotlight/Nick Jr.
New York   London   Toronto   Sydney

Hi! I am  .
DORA

Today  and I
BOOTS

are at the  .
BEACH

Oh, no! is caught in a .

He needs our help!

We need something

to cut through the 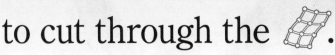.

We can look in .
BACKPACK

Do you see something

that can cut through the  ?
NET

These  SCISSORS

can cut through the NET !

 has a  .

BABY CRAB   SHELL NECKLACE

He wants to give it

to  .

MAMI CRAB

But he cannot find her.

We can help him

find .

MAMI CRAB

is on CRAB ISLAND.

MAMI CRAB

To get to ,

CRAB ISLAND

we need to go through

the

SAND CASTLE

and over the .

SNAPPING CLAMS

Come on!

We made it to the .
SAND CASTLE

What a nice  !
SAND CASTLE

I wonder who lives here.

The  lives here! The SQUISHY SQUID likes to play music.

SQUISHY SQUID

To go through the ,
SAND CASTLE

we have to sing and dance

to the  's song.
SQUISHY SQUID

We did it!

We made it through

the  .
SAND CASTLE

Great!

Where do we go next?

Yeah!

We go over the .

SNAPPING CLAMS

The  are big.

And they snap!

How do we get over them

without getting snapped?

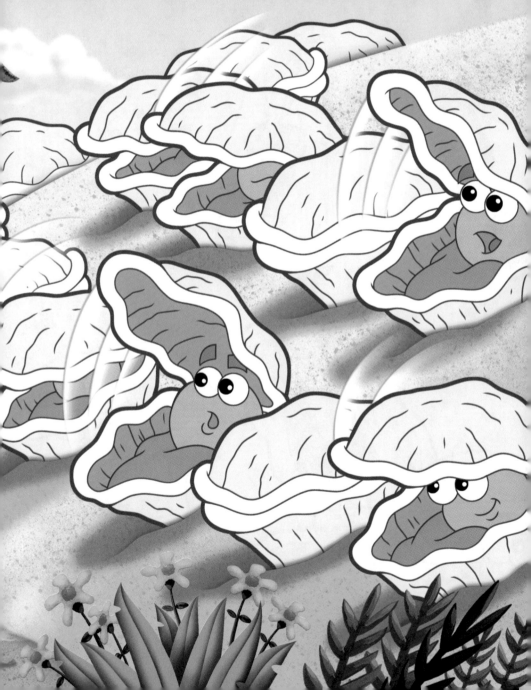

When the  snap,

SNAPPING CLAMS

we have to jump.

Jump!

Jump!

Jump over the  !

SNAPPING CLAMS

Look! There is  .
CRAB ISLAND

We can use this
BOAT

to get there.

Uh-oh.

The are missing!
OARS

We cannot paddle the
BOAT

without  .
OARS

can help us.

BABY CRAB

He is pulling the !

BOAT

Wow, he is pulling fast!

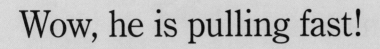 is strong.

BABY CRAB

We made it to  !

CRAB ISLAND

 loves the .

MAMI CRAB   SHELL NECKLACE

She loves 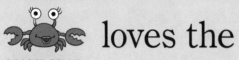 , too!

BABY CRAB

The Rainforest Race

adapted by Lara Bergen

based on the teleplay by Rosemary Contreras

illustrated by Corey Wolfe and Art Mawhinney

Ready-to-Read

Simon Spotlight/ Nick Jr.

New York   London   Toronto   Sydney

Hi, I am !
DIEGO

Today is the Rainforest Race!

I love races!

Do you?

There are animal teams from all over the rainforest. There is a  team,

SPECTACLED BEAR

a team,

HOWLER MONKEY

and a team.

PUMA

The winner of the race will get a big, blue .

RIBBON

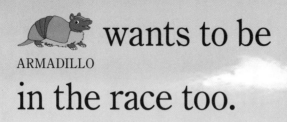 wants to be

ARMADILLO

in the race too.

But she does not have

a team.

I know.

I will join her team!

ARMADILLO is worried.
The other animals are bigger.

But has a strong shell.
ARMADILLO

She has sharp claws.

And she can roll into a .
BALL

The other animals cannot

do that!

It is time to start the race!

We need to go to the

shaky ,

NUT TREES

the muddy slide,

MUD

and the big .

MOUNTAIN

Ready, set, go!

Here are the shaky  !

NUT TREES

The  are slowing

NUTS

the big animals down.

But 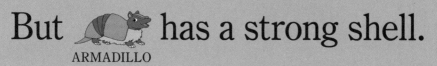 has a strong shell.
ARMADILLO

The 🌰 do not stop her.
NUTS

Go, 🦔, go!
ARMADILLO

Now we are at
the muddy  slide.
MUD
The , the ,
PUMAS   SPECTACLED BEARS
and the slide down.
HOWLER MONKEYS

Oh, no!

 cannot slide.

ARMADILLO

Her short legs are stuck

in the  .

MUD

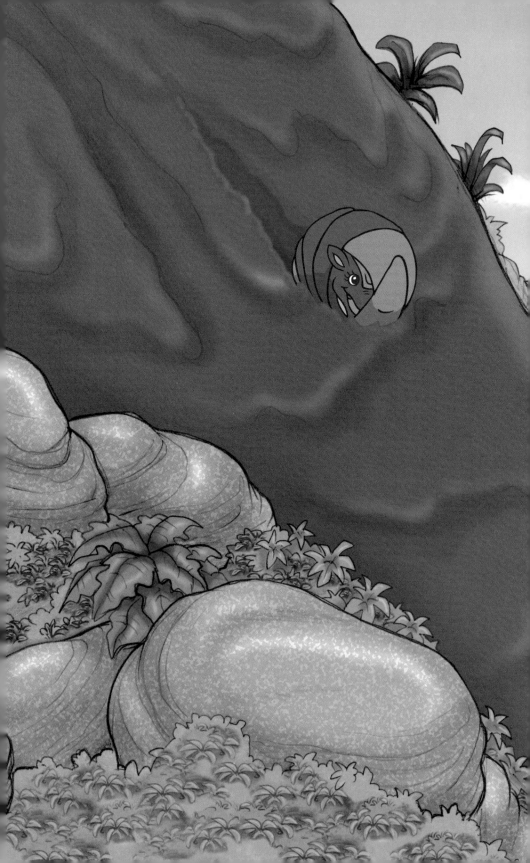

But can roll into a .

ARMADILLO
BALL

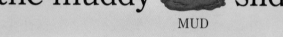 can roll down

ARMADILLO

the muddy ⬛ slide.

MUD

Roll, 🦡, roll!

ARMADILLO

We made it to the big  .
MOUNTAIN
The other teams are
at the top.

 is at the bottom.
ARMADILLO

Her legs are too short.

It is hard for her

to climb the .
MOUNTAIN

I know how to get to the other side of the !

MOUNTAIN

 has sharp claws.

ARMADILLO

She can dig a !

TUNNEL

Dig,  , dig!

ARMADILLO

We are almost there!

We made it to the  !
FINISH LINE

Here come the other animals.

They can run fast.

But ARMADILLO can roll faster.

Roll,  , roll!
ARMADILLO

Roll across the  .
FINISH LINE

We did it!

We won the Rainforest Race!

Everyone gets a big  .

RIBBON

Hooray for teamwork!

Around the World!

adapted by Suzanne D. Nimm
based on the original teleplay written by Valerie Walsh
illustrated by Ron Zalme

Ready-to-Read

Simon Spotlight/Nick Jr.
New York   London   Toronto   Sydney

Hi! I am  DORA .

Today is Friendship Day!

 swiped all

of the friendship  !

Now we have to return them

to our friends around the !

Will you help us

deliver the friendship ?
BRACELETS

Great!

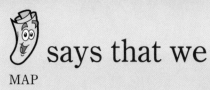 says that we

have to bring

to our friends

at the  in France,

the  in Tanzania,

MOUNTAIN

the ⌂ in Russia,

PALACE

and the Great ≈ of China.

WALL

We are in France!

Where is the Eiffel ?

TOWER

We have to follow the road with  **DIAMONDS** to get to the Eiffel **TOWER**. Do you see **DIAMONDS**?

Fifi the  will try
SKUNK

to swipe our ⬭ !
BRACELETS

Do you see a 🦨 ?
SKUNK

Oh, no! Say "No swiping!"

Thanks for stopping the !

SKUNK

Now our friends in France

can get friendship .

BRACELETS

We are in Tanzania!

This  is giving us
ELEPHANT

a ride to the .
MOUNTAIN

Look! I see a  and a .
ZEBRA   LION

Uh-oh! Sami the will try

to swipe the friendship .

BRACELETS

If you see a , say

"No swiping!"

All of our friends

are so happy

to get their  !

BRACELETS

Next we have to ride

in a 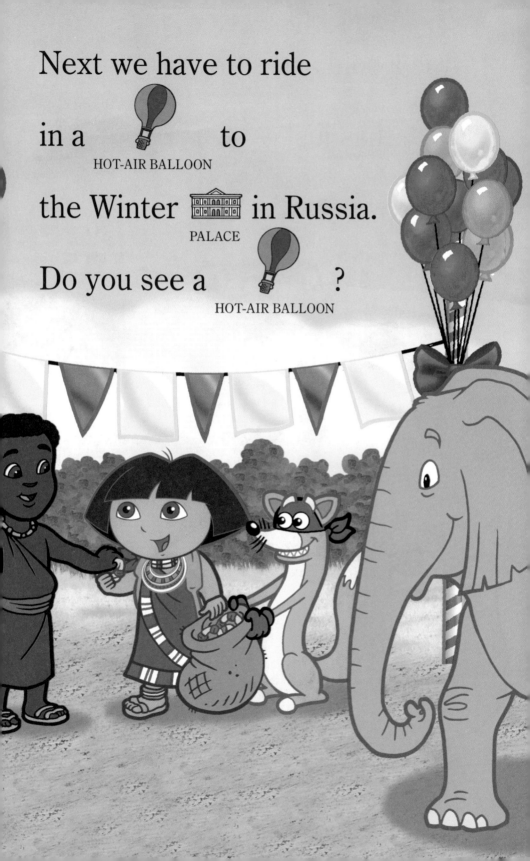 to
HOT-AIR BALLOON

the Winter 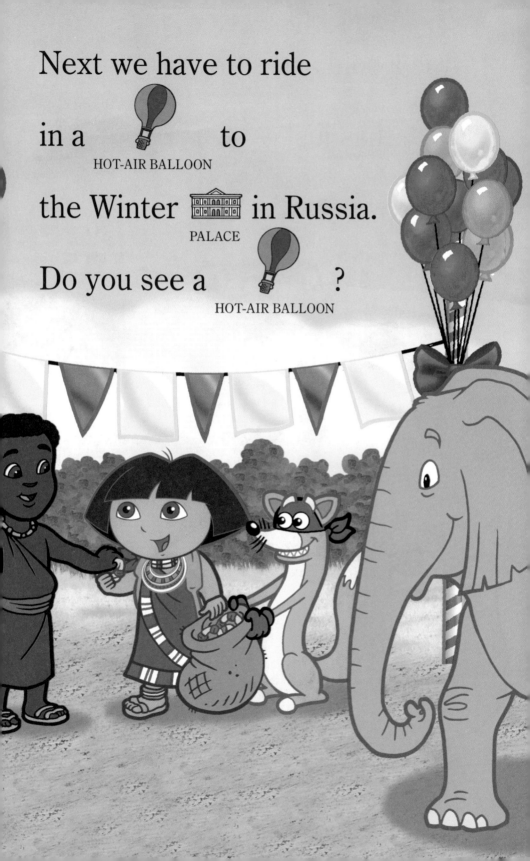 in Russia.
PALACE

Do you see a 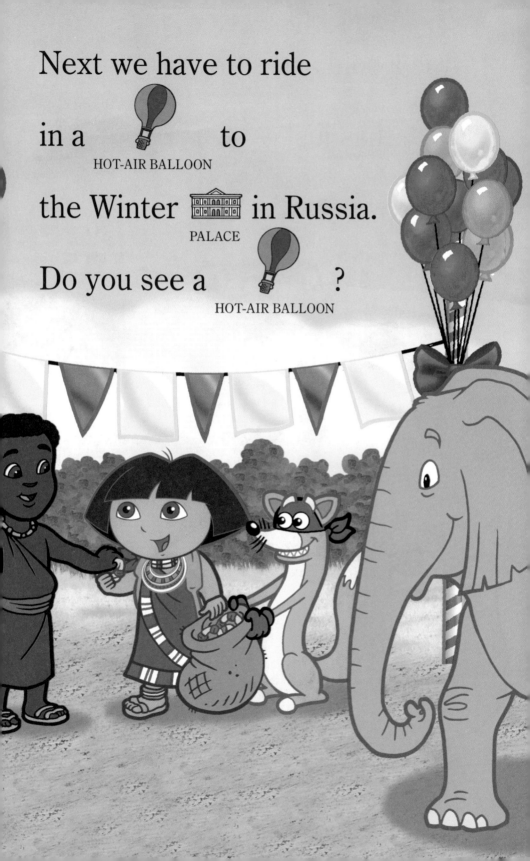 ?
HOT-AIR BALLOON

It is a cold and snowy day.

 has just

what we need!

Do you see a  , ,
COAT   MITTENS

a , and ?
HAT   SKIS

Now we can give out

friendship 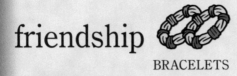 BRACELETS

to our friends in Russia.

Look! One is different

from the other SNOWMAN .

Wait—it is Fomkah the

sneaky  !

BEAR

Fomkah wants to swipe

the friendship  .

BRACELETS

Say "No swiping!"

Now we can give out

the 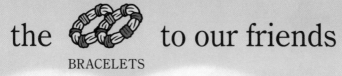 to our friends
BRACELETS

at the Great of China.
WALL

Ying-Ying the
WEASEL

will try to swipe the .
BRACELETS

Say "No swiping!"

Look! There is one  left.

BRACELET

It is a friendship for !

BRACELET SWIPER

Now everyone has a .

BRACELET

Thank you for helping us

deliver the friendship
BRACELETS

to all our friends around the !
WORLD

Happy Friendship Day!

Diego's Birthday Surprise

by Lara Bergen
illustrated by Art Mawhinney

Ready-to-Read

Simon Spotlight/Nick Jr.
New York   London   Toronto   Sydney

Hi! My name is .

 DIEGO

This is .

ALICIA

Do you know what today is?

It is 's birthday!

BABY JAGUAR

We will have a party.

It will be a surprise party!

 has a of all of the

ALICIA   LIST

things we need.

First on the list is 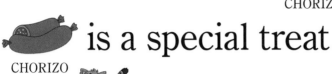.
CHORIZO

 is a special treat
CHORIZO

for .
BABY JAGUAR

He loves to eat meat.

What else is on the ?
We need party , ,

HATS   PRESENTS

LIST

and  .

BALLOONS

PARTY LIST

Chorizo

Party hats

Presents

Balloons

We have .

CHORIZO

We have party snacks for everyone!

We have party HATS.

We have  .
PRESENTS

But where are the 🎈 ?
BALLOONS

Look out the  !

WINDOW

The  BOBOS have the BALLOONS !

Say "Freeze,  !"
BOBOS
Oops!

The  **BOBOS** let the **BALLOONS** go!

They are sorry.

Hurry! We have to get the  BALLOONS back! BABY JAGUAR will be at the ANIMAL RESCUE CENTER soon!

 can help us find

the .

Just say " 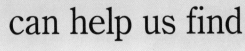 !"

 will zoom through the

CLICK

 to look for the .

RAINFOREST   BALLOONS

Are these  ?

BALLOONS

No, those are .

FLOWERS

Are these ?

BALLOONS

Yes!

The  are up in the .

BALLOONS   TREE

can help us

RESCUE PACK

get up the   to the

TREE   BALLOONS

Can we use a 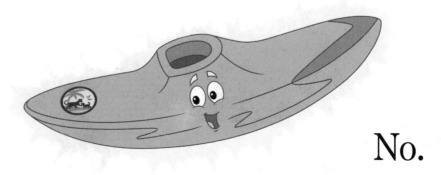 to

KAYAK

reach the top of the ? TREE

No.

Can we climb a to

LADDER

reach the top of the ? TREE

Yes!

Hooray!

We did it!

We got the  !

BALLOONS

Look! It is .

ALICIA

We need to hurry.

 is coming!

BABY JAGUAR

Let's go!

We have to get the  BALLOONS

back to the ANIMAL RESCUE CENTER

fast.

Yeah!

We made it just in time.

Surprise!

Happy birthday, !

BABY JAGUAR

Dora's Sleepover

by Lara Bergen
illustrated by Victoria Miller

Ready-to-Read

Simon Spotlight/Nick Jr.

New York   London   Toronto   Sydney

Hi! I am .
DORA

It is a big night!

I am having a sleepover

with my best friend, ,

BOOTS

at his !

TREE HOUSE

First I need to pack  .

BACKPACK

Do you see what I should

pack?

I will take my ,
PAJAMAS

my , my ,
FLASHLIGHT   SLEEPING BAG

and my of stories.
BOOK   PIRATE

loves stories!

BOOTS   PIRATE

has made some COOKIES for BOOTS and me. Yum! MAMI puts the COOKIES in a BASKET.

Do **you** like ?
COOKIES

Thank you, .
MAMI

Good-bye!

How do we get
to 's TREE HOUSE ?
BOOTS   TREE HOUSE

MAP can show us

the way.

We go through the ,
TUNNEL

then through the ,
JUNGLE

and that's how we get to

BOOTS   TREE HOUSE

We made it to the  .
TUNNEL

But the  is **so** dark!
TUNNEL

Is there something in my 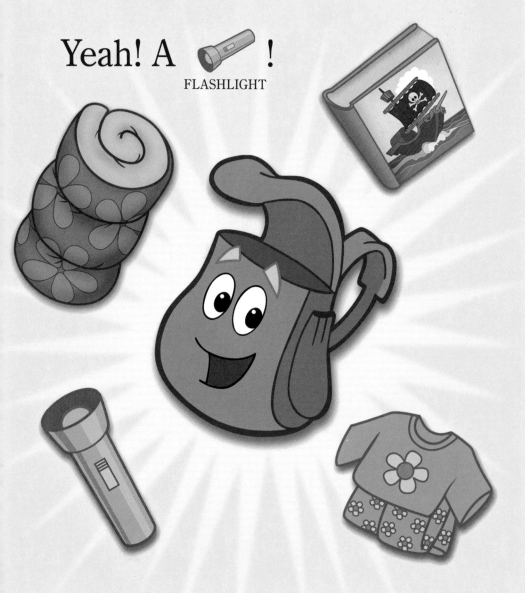 BACKPACK that will

help us see in the dark?

Yeah! A 🔦 !

FLASHLIGHT

We made it through the .
TUNNEL

Now we need to go

through the .
JUNGLE

Uh-oh! Do you see

someone behind that ?
TREE

It is  !
SWIPER

 wants to swipe our
SWIPER

 of .
BASKET   COOKIES

Say " , no swiping!"
SWIPER

We stopped .
SWIPER

And there is 's  !
BOOTS   TREE HOUSE

We can climb the
LADDER

to get to 's .
BOOTS   TREE HOUSE

Hi,  ! I am ready

for our sleepover!

I have my ,

PAJAMAS

my FLASHLIGHT, my SLEEPING BAG,

my BOOK of PIRATE stories,

and a BASKET of COOKIES

from MAMI!

It is time to put on our .

PAJAMAS

Then we can turn on our

 and eat the .

FLASHLIGHTS   COOKIES

Yum!

I can read my
BOOK

of 🏴‍☠️ stories
PIRATE

to 🐵 too.
BOOTS

Look at the 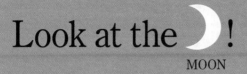!
MOON

The is so big and bright.
MOON

 yawns.
BOOTS

 is sleepy.
BOOTS

I am sleepy too.

We get into our .

SLEEPING BAGS

Good night, .

BOOTS

And good night

to you, too!

Diego Saves the Tree Frogs

adapted by Sarah Willson
based on the original teleplay by Madellaine Paxson
illustrated by Susan Hall

Ready-to-Read

SIMON SPOTLIGHT/NICK JR.
New York   London   Toronto   Sydney

Hi! I am .

DIEGO

This is .

BABY JAGUAR

I hear some .

TREE FROGS

They need our help!

Hi,  !

ALICIA

 is my sister.

ALICIA

Hurry,  !

ALICIA

Tell us about  .

TREE FROGS

 live

in the rainforest.

Some

have eyes.

RED

TREE FROGS have strong **LEGS**.

Their **LEGS** help them

to jump high.

TREE FROGS have sticky .
TOES

Their help them
TOES

to climb.

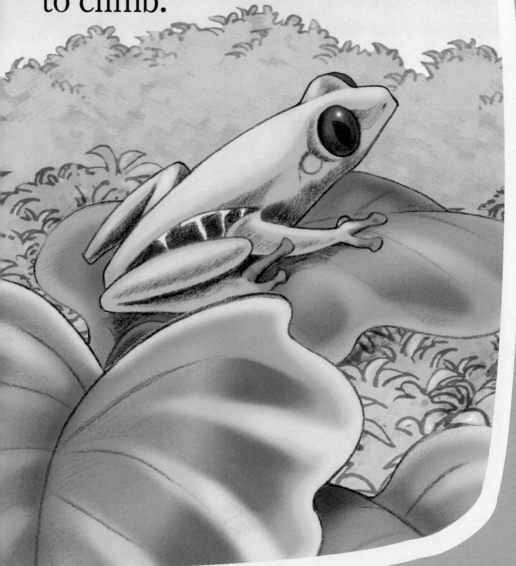

is our camera.

CLICK

 found the  !

CLICK   TREE FROGS

Do you see the ?

TREE FROGS

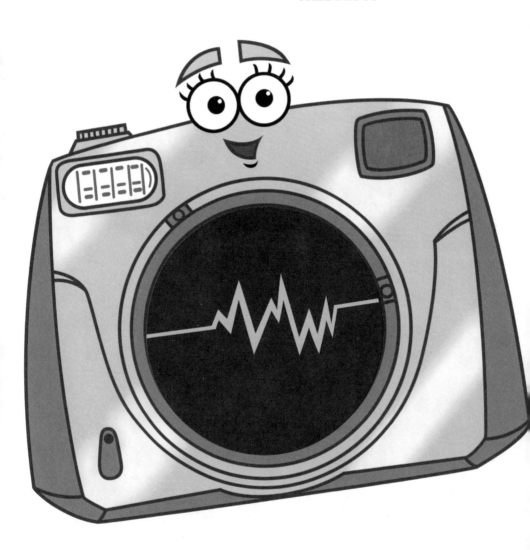

The  fell!
TREE FROGS

They are on a ⟋.
BRANCH

The ⟋ is in the ∽!
BRANCH   RIVER

Come on. We need to save

the !

TREE FROGS

Look out for the  !
COCONUTS

Jump like a .
TREE FROG

Jump over the !
COCONUTS

The went

TREE FROGS

into the 🔺.

PYRAMID

How will we get inside?

Do you see a 🚪?

DOOR

I need my sticky .
GLOVES

My  help me climb
GLOVES

like a .
TREE FROG

We made it!

Do you see the 🐸? TREE FROGS

Oh, no! The  !

WATERFALL

Tell the

TREE FROGS

to jump!

The  jumped.

TREE FROGS

They are safe.

I will take them home.

ALICIA found a new TREE for the TREE FROGS.

The new  TREE is strong.
The new TREE is safe.

The  are happy.

TREE FROGS

They love their new .

TREE